by Diana G. Gallagher

illustrated by Brann Garvey

HIRED or FIRED?

Claudia Cristina Cortez is published by Stone Arch Books
151 Good Counsel Drive, P.O. Box 669
Mankato, Minnesota 56002
www.stonearchbooks.com

Library of Congress Cataloging-in-Publication Data
Gallagher, Diana G.
  Hired or fired? / by Diana G. Gallagher ; illustrated by Brann Garvey.
     p. cm. — (Claudia Cristina Cortez)
  ISBN 978-1-4342-1574-1
  [1. Work—Fiction. 2. Middle schools—Fiction. 3. Schools—Fiction.
4. Hispanic Americans—Fiction.] I. Garvey, Brann, ill. II. Title.
  PZ7.G13543Hi 2010
  [Fic]—dc22
                                    2009002545

Summary: All the seventh graders have to find jobs for Work Week. Claudia's job
should be a piece of cake, but starting on day one, she feels like she's messing up.
Can she figure out how to keep her job, or will Claudia be the first person ever to
fail Work Week?

Creative Director: Heather Kindseth
Graphic Designer: Carla Zetina-Yglesias

Photo Credits
Delaney Photography, cover

Printed in the United States of America

Table of Contents

Cast of

CLAUDIA

ME

That's me. I'm thirteen, and I'm in the seventh grade at Pine Tree Middle School. I live with my mom, my dad, and my brother, Jimmy. I have one cat, Ping-Ping. I like music, baseball, and hanging out with my friends.

MONICA

MONICA is my very best friend. We met when we were really little, and we've been best friends ever since. I don't know what I'd do without her! Monica loves horses. In fact, when she grows up, she wants to be an Olympic rider!

BECCA

BECCA is one of my closest friends. She lives next door to Monica. Becca is really, really smart. She gets good grades. She's also really good at art.

ADAM

ADAM and I met when we were in third grade. Now that we're teenagers, we don't spend as much time together as we did when we were kids, but he's always there for me when I need him. (Plus, he's the only person who wants to talk about baseball with me!)

Characters

TOMMY's our class clown. Sometimes he's really funny, but sometimes he is just annoying. Becca has a crush on him . . . but I'd never tell.

I think **PETER** is probably the smartest person I've ever met. Seriously. He's even smarter than our teachers! He's also one of my friends. Which is lucky, because sometimes he helps me with homework.

Every school has a bully, and **JENNY** is ours. She's the tallest person in our class, and the meanest, too. She always threatens to stomp people. No one's ever seen her stomp anyone, but that doesn't mean it hasn't happened!

ANNA is the most popular girl at our school. Everyone wants to be friends with her. I think that's weird, because Anna can be really, really mean. I mostly try to stay away from her.

Cast of

CARLY is Anna's best friend. She always tries to act exactly like Anna does. She even wears the exact same clothes. She's never really been mean to me, but she's never been nice to me either!

CARLY

NICK is my annoying seven-year-old neighbor. I get stuck babysitting him a lot. He likes to make me miserable. (Okay, he's not that bad ALL of the time . . . just most of the time.)

NICK

DAD

Besides being my **DAD**, Dad is also the owner and manager of Cortez Computers. His computer store sells computers, software, and office supplies. I think my dad would be a good boss, and now I'll find out for myself!

Characters

JIMMY is my older brother. He's a true computer genius. He ignores me most of the time, but that's what big brothers are for.

JIMMY

MR. DRAKE works for my dad at Cortez Computers. He is a really good salesperson, but he doesn't know a whole lot about computers.

MR. DRAKE

MS. STARK is my homeroom teacher at school. She's pretty nice, but she doesn't let us get away with much!

MS. STARK

MOM is great at giving me advice. She helps me with all of my problems. She's also a pretty good cook!

MOM

CHAPTER 1

GET A JOB

The Pine Tree Middle School day always began in Homeroom. First **Ms. Stark** took attendance. When she called our names, we were supposed to reply, "Here!"

Tommy, our class clown, always said, "There!" when Ms. Stark called his name. **He never did things like everyone else.** Tommy thought being an oddball was funny.

After attendance, **Principal Paul** talked on the PA system.

Typical Morning Announcements

1. Lunch menu

Mr. Paul's favorite food joke: "That's split pea soup, not spit pea soup."

2. Sports practice and event schedules

Mr. Paul's favorite sports joke: "We're having a pep rally this afternoon, not a pet rally. **No dogs allowed**."

3. Club meeting changes and reminders

Mr. Paul's favorite club joke: "All clubs must be approved, including **golf clubs** and **club sandwiches**."

We had heard his lame jokes a thousand times, but we always laughed anyway.

Then Principal Paul made an extra announcement.

"Next week is a big week for the seventh graders at Pine Tree Middle School," he began.

My friends and I looked at each other.

"It's **Work Week**!" Principal Paul said.

Everyone in my homeroom started cheering and talking.

"That's enough," Ms. Stark said. She handed each of us a packet of papers.

"Here's the list of jobs," she said. "Now, don't spend all day discussing it. **You can talk about it at lunch.**"

It was the only thing we talked about at lunch that day. Most kids were excited, but not all of us were.

"*I don't want a job!*" **Jenny Pinski** yelled, stomping through the cafeteria. Everyone jumped out of her way.

But even the school bully didn't have a choice. Every seventh grader had to get a job.

"What if nobody wants a SHORT guy?" **Larry Kyle** asked.

"You're tall enough to ride the Sky High roller coaster," Adam pointed out. **Adam** was one of my best friends, and he loved the amusement park.

"And it's **illegal** to not hire someone for **stupid reasons** like their height," I told Larry. My dad owned a computer store, so I knew about that stuff.

"I get to pick my job first," **Anna Dunlap** said, looking at the list of jobs.

Anna was so **popular** and bossy no one would challenge her. "I'll let you know what job I want as soon as I decide," she added.

"There are dozens of jobs!" Becca said, running her finger down the list. "I don't know how I'll decide." **Becca** was another one of my best friends. "What are you going to do, Claudia?" she asked.

"I don't know," I told her. I started to feel **nervous**.

It was Monday. We had to be employed by Friday. First we had to follow three steps:

1. Write a résumé

2. Go for an interview

3. Get hired

"What if the place where we want to work isn't on the list?" **Peter** asked. He was the smartest kid in school. He could be a **rocket scientist**, but our town didn't have a space program.

"We can work anywhere," **Monica** explained, "as long as it's a real store or company."

"I wish we could just mow lawns or babysit," I said. I already had lawnmowing, weed-picking, dog-walking, and babysitting customers. I liked doing jobs like that. **I liked being my own boss.**

For the Work Week project, someone else would be my boss, and I wasn't sure how I felt about that. Then I had a great idea. I knew that lots of people were their own bosses. Like my **dad**. He owned his own business. **Maybe I could do that too!**

Ms. Stark walked by just then. "Hey, Ms. Stark," I said. "I have **my own business** running errands and doing chores for my neighbors. Can't I be self-employed for Work Week?"

"Sorry, Claudia," Ms. Stark said. "It's GREAT that you have your own business, but for the Work Week project, you have to get a grade. And the grade comes from your employee evaluation at the end of the week. *You can't give yourself an evaluation.* It wouldn't be fair."

I'm always **honest**, so I wouldn't give myself a good evaluation if I didn't deserve it. But I knew Ms. Stark was right. "Okay," I said sadly.

"I'm sure you'll find a job on the list," Ms. Stark said. She smiled and then walked away.

"I want to do something I like," Adam said. **"Then it won't seem like work."**

"That's why I want a job at Earth First, the environmental science lab," Peter said.

"Earth First **isn't on the list**," Becca pointed out.

"But if they offer you a job, I'm sure the school will okay it," I told Peter. **I try to look on the bright side.** There almost always is one.

"Having fun would be cool," **Tommy** said. "But the best part of Work Week is less homework."

Most teachers don't give homework during Work Week, but *it's not a rule*. Some of the **tough** teachers still do.

"The best part is the paycheck," Larry said. All of the employers were **required** to pay us minimum wage. I hadn't decided yet what to spend my earnings on.

"I found **the perfect job!**" Becca exclaimed. She read from the list. "Assistant art teacher at Pine Tree Elementary."

"Perfect," I said. Becca wanted to be an artist. And she loved kids.

"The Harmon County Hawks need a water boy," Adam said. The Hawks were his **favorite** baseball team. "I'm going to apply right after school."

"What do you want to do, Tommy?" Becca asked.

I was curious too. Tommy loves to make people LAUGH. What kind of job would he want?

"I want to be a stand-up comedian or an actor," Tommy said. "There's nothing on this list for me."

"Horseback rider isn't on the list either," Monica said.

"There must be something you can do with horses," I said. Monica was born with **horse fever**. She loved everything that has anything to do with horses.

"Attention!" **Anna** yelled. She stood up. "I'm going to get the display designer job at Fiona's Fashions." She scanned the room and caught me watching her. "Don't you **dare** go after my job, Claudia," she warned me.

"Don't worry," I told her. "That doesn't sound like a good job to me."

I wasn't afraid of Anna, and I didn't care what she thought. I didn't want to design fashion displays.

The problem was, I didn't want any of the jobs on the list. I was an **entrepreneur**. That's a word for a person who starts and runs a business.

Doing little jobs to earn money was **my idea**. I found my own customers, and I was responsible when something went wrong. I also got to keep all of the money I made.

I didn't want to work for someone else.

CHAPTER 2

WHY ME?

Monica and Becca **promised** to come over after school. We were going to work on our résumés together.

My seven-year-old neighbor, Nick, and I waited for my friends in the tree house in my back yard. I had to watch him while Mom went shopping.

Nick lifted a bench seat and pulled out a box of plastic bricks. I keep toys, books, magazines, and craft supplies inside the benches that line the walls of the tree house.

"I'm 𝒯𝐻𝐼𝑅𝒮𝒯𝒴," Nick said.

I said, "We'll have juice when Monica and Becca get here."

That was **Mistake #1**. I should have said, "Okay," and given him a juice box.

"I'm thirsty **now**!" Nick said. He stamped his foot and dumped the box of bricks.

I said, "They'll be here soon."

That was **Mistake #2**. I should have said, "Okay," and given him a juice box.

"I'll kick these bricks," Nick said. He glared at me.

I said, "Go ahead, but then you can't have juice."

That was **Mistake #3**. I should have said, "My friends are late," and given him a juice box.

Nick pulled his foot back.

"Don't do that," I said.

If Nick kicked the bricks, I absolutely could not give him juice. He wouldn't believe I meant what I said ever again.

But not giving him juice might be worse.

No juice = kicking, screaming tantrum

Tantrum = too much noise to think

Can't think = can't write = no résumé

Luckily, Monica and Becca climbed into the tree house just in time.

"They're here," Nick said. He held out his hand. "Juice time."

I gave him a juice box.

"We brought chocolate chip cookies," Becca said.

"**FANTASTIC!**" I said. Juice, cookies, and building bricks would keep Nick happy and quiet.

Becca, Monica, and I sat down with our notebooks.

"How important is a résumé?" Monica asked.

"**Very important,**" Becca said. "It tells an employer all about you."

"If the employer likes it," I added, "they'll call you for an interview."

"Can't I just show up and ask for a job?" Monica asked.

"Sure, but you still need a résumé," I said. "We have to give Ms. Stark a copy, too. It's part of our grade."

We wrote our **names, addresses, and phone numbers** at the top of our papers. My dad calls that "contact information."

"What else?" Monica asked.

"List anything that explains why you're perfect for the job," I said.

"That's **EASY**," Becca said. She wrote down that she was a babysitter, and she listed her customers. That proved she got along with kids. "I'll take some of my artwork to my interview to **prove my artistic ability**," she told us.

"Is my résumé too **short**?" Monica asked. She held up her sheet of paper. "I only have two things to list."

I read Monica's résumé. She had written that she loved horses, and that she took riding lessons. She was applying for a job as a sales clerk at the Tack Shop. The store  at the mall sold riding clothes and horse supplies.

"I think that's enough," I said.

I listed all of my jobs on my resume. "I hope my customers are **good references**," I said. "I don't want anyone to say anything bad about me."

"What's a reference?" Nick asked.

"A reference is someone an employer can call to ask if you're a good worker," Monica explained.

"And if you're **honest and nice**," Becca added.

"Don't let anybody call me, Claudia," 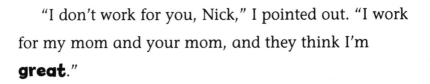 Nick said. "I'll tell them all that you're mean."

"I don't work for you, Nick," I pointed out. "I work for my mom and your mom, and they think I'm **great**."

My other customers did too.

I probably wouldn't need references though. Since I had to get a job, there was only **one place** I wanted to work.

For my **dad**, at Cortez Computers.

CHAPTER 3

FACE TO FACE

I loved my dad, but we never agreed about anything.

For example:

Dad hated Bad Dog, my all–time favorite band. He wouldn't let me play their CDs in the car. And I couldn't play them loud in my room.

I thought music was **way better** if it was **way louder.**

Dad thought going to the movies was a waste of money. He always said that I should just be **patient** and wait until the movie came out on DVD.

I thought movies were way better on big theater screens than on tiny TVs.

Dad was CONVINCED I could get straight As if I didn't spend so much time:

Reading novels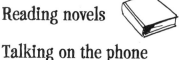

Talking on the phone

Having fun

I got good grades. They just weren't perfect.

My dad didn't understand my older brother, Jimmy, either, except for one thing. **They both loved computers.**

Jimmy had worked at Dad's store during his seventh-grade Work Week project a few years ago. After that, he started working at Cortez Computers every Wednesday afternoon after school, and sometimes on Saturdays.

Jimmy was **a computer whiz** and **a video game expert**. The customers loved him.

Dad beamed with pride whenever Jimmy got a compliment. Jimmy got lots of compliments at work, so **Dad beamed with pride a lot**. And at home, he'd sometimes tell my mom about how great Jimmy had been at the store that day.

I wanted my dad to be proud of **me**.

I knew that I had to work at Cortez Computers too. That way, my dad would see that I was **just as smart** and serious as my big brother.

I called Dad at the store on Tuesday after school. "The seventh grade Work Week project starts Monday," I told him.

"Have you found a job?" **Dad** asked.

"Not yet," I answered. "I want to work at your store."

SILENCE.

Uh-oh! What if my father didn't want to hire me?

"I have a résumé and references," I added.

"Have Mom fax them over," Dad said. "I'll give you an *interview* when I get home."

Asking anyone for a job is hard. Asking my dad is harder. I went to ask my mother for advice.

"Can you give me any tips for my interview?" I asked her.

"Think before you speak," **Mom** said. "Sometimes you're too **impulsive**."

She was right about that! Once I blurted out, "You've got a bald spot!" I forgot Dad worried about losing his hair.

"And sometimes you talk too much," Mom reminded me.

That was true most of the time. When Dad made me nervous, **I babbled**. He hated that. He liked people to say what they mean and not use **a million words** to do it.

"Thanks, Mom," I told her.

When Dad got home from work, he and I sat down in the living room. He had scribbled notes on my résumé.

That made me worry.

Résumé Worries

Did I misspell something?

Did I write down the wrong phone numbers for my references?

What if my job experience wasn't good enough?

What if it didn't look professional enough?

I wanted to ask if everything was okay, but I waited quietly.

Dad cleared his throat.

I held my breath.

"I called your customers," Dad said. "Everyone thinks you're an EXCELLENT worker."

"Cool!" I exclaimed. **Oops.** That wasn't very professional. "I'm so pleased," I said.

"Can you work and keep up with school?" Dad asked.

"Yes," I said. "Working is a school project, and we won't have as much homework during Work Week."

"I see," Dad said. He nodded. "Why do  you want to work at Cortez Computers?"

I was ready for that one. "I want to learn the family business," I told him.

Dad smiled. "I didn't know you were interested in the store," he said. "I'll have to think about this. I'll decide and let you know on Friday morning."

"Okay," I said.

I crossed my fingers hopefully. Friday was the deadline to get a job. **I didn't want to be the only seventh grader who was unemployed.**

CHAPTER 4

YOU'RE HIRED

On Friday morning, I *HURRIED* to get ready. Then I ran into the kitchen.

"Where's Dad?" I asked my mom, who was standing at the stove, stirring a big pot of oatmeal.

"He's already at work," Mom said.

"But he's supposed to tell me if I got the job!" I said. **I was starting to feel frantic.** What if he'd decided not to hire me? What if he'd forgotten that I even applied for the job?

Just then, the phone rang. My mom answered it. "It's for you, honey," she said, handing me the phone.

That was **weird**. Who was calling me before school?

"Hello, Ms. Cortez," a man's voice said. "This is Eduardo Cortez at Cortez Computers."

I gulped. "Hi **Dad**," I said. "I mean, Mr. Cortez."

"I'm calling to let you know that *we've decided to hire you for the job*," Dad said.

I thought fast. How would a **professional** person react?

"Thank you very much, sir," I said calmly. After I hung up, I yelled, **"Yay! I got the job!"**

Mom smiled. "You better get a move on," she told me. "You're going to be late for school."

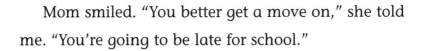

In Homeroom, everyone had to give a job search report.

Becca went first. "The art teacher at Pine Tree Elementary interviewed me yesterday," she said.

"Did Ms. Fong **hire you?**" **Ms. Stark** asked.

"**Yes,**" Becca said. "I brought babysitting references and some artwork. That convinced her I could help little kids."

Ms. Stark called on Adam next.

"I don't have the job I wanted," Adam said. **"Brad does."**

I muffled a gasp. I couldn't believe that Brad  Turino would steal Adam's job. Brad was **too cute and nice** to be a jerk.

"The Harmon County Hawks wanted one water boy," Adam went on. "**Brad got there first.** First come, first served."

That explained it. Brad didn't do anything mean, and Adam wasn't mad. **I was so relieved.** I didn't have to choose between one of my best friends and the guy I secretly had a crush on.

"Did you find something else, Adam?" Ms. Stark asked.

Adam nodded. "Junior sports reporter at the *Harmon County Herald*," he said.

Monica got the sales clerk job at the Tack Shop.

Earth First, the environmental science lab, created a **special position** for **Peter**. He'd gotten the job approved by Principal Paul and Ms. Stark.

The Coffee Café hired Sylvia to be a waitress.

"I'll be at the Million Movie video store," Jenny said. "They don't really have a MILLION DVDs. But I can watch all the new releases while I'm there."

Ms. Stark pointed to Tommy.

"I applied for a job," Tommy said, "but I don't know if I got it. I have to call after school to find out."

Anna waved her hand. "I'm the new display designer and **teen wardrobe consultant** at Fiona Fashions," she said proudly. "The owner hired me on the spot. She didn't have to think about it. Isn't that amazing?"

"You're going to sell clothes," Jenny said. **"Big deal."**

Anna's cheeks turned red and her eyes bulged, but she didn't argue. No one argues with Jenny Pinski.

"What about you, **Carly**?" Ms. Stark asked.

"I'm selling popcorn and candy at the movie theater," Carly said.

"Are you employed, Claudia?" Ms. Stark asked.

The bell rang just as I started to answer. Everyone stood up to leave for first period.

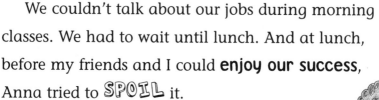

I gave a short, speedy report as I walked toward the door. "I'm going to be working at Cortez Computers," I said.

We couldn't talk about our jobs during morning classes. We had to wait until lunch. And at lunch, before my friends and I could **enjoy our success**, Anna tried to SPOIL it.

"Did you apply to be the new **Quick Burger clown**?" Anna asked Tommy.

A class clown fools around and tells jokes. The Quick Burger clown wears a purple wig, gigantic floppy shoes, and a polka dot suit.

I knew Anna was trying to hurt Tommy's feelings. Luckily, he didn't let her bother him.

"Nope. Quick Burger isn't my STYLE," Tommy said. "I auditioned to help host a drive-time radio show on WHCR."

"Oh, that's so EXCITING," Becca gushed. She has a secret crush on Tommy.

"Yeah," Tommy agreed. "I hope I get it."

"You will," Becca said.

Anna didn't look happy. She thought she had 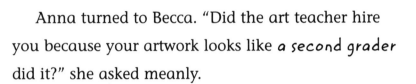 the best job. But radio star beat fashion consultant by a mile.

Anna turned to Becca. "Did the art teacher hire you because your artwork looks like *a second grader* did it?" she asked meanly.

"No," Becca said. "But I did show Ms. Fong artwork I did when I was in second grade. I keep all of my good pieces."

Next Anna tried to insult Adam. "Too bad you got stuck with your **second-choice job**," she said. "But that's better than sticking the Harmon County Hawks with the **second-best water boy**."

"I get to watch next week's Hawks game from the press booth," Adam said.

"That's okay if you like **stupid things** like baseball," Anna said. She shrugged, but she wasn't done. She looked around the room for her next victim.

Anna spotted Sylvia next. Anna turned to her and said, "I hope you don't get fired for being a slowpoke, Sylvia. Your Coffee Café customers might complain if their food is cold. *Then you'll get fired.*"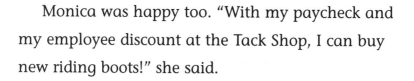

"Waitresses get tips," Sylvia said. "I'll move fast for money."

Everyone was trying to ignore Anna.

"The environmental lab wants to hire me as an intern when I'm sixteen," Peter said. "Only two years, seven months, and eleven days to go. *I can't wait.*"

Monica was happy too. "With my paycheck and my employee discount at the Tack Shop, I can buy new riding boots!" she said.

Anna was striking out. Everyone had a job they really liked. There was no one left to pick on — **except me.**

"Did you beg your father for a job because no one else would hire you, Claudia?" Anna asked, smiling. She raised her eyebrows. I could tell that she was so sure she had zinged me.

I didn't care what Anna thought. I cared what my father thought. I was glad he had given me a job. But if I **messed up**, he'd never take me seriously.

And that was **the whole point** of working at Cortez Computers.

CHAPTER 5

FIRST DAY FLUBS

Every student had the same work schedule: two hours after school Monday through Friday, and four hours on Saturday.

On Monday morning, I had **first-day-on-the-job jitters.**

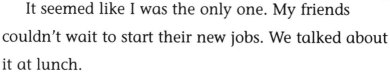

It seemed like I was the only one. My friends couldn't wait to start their new jobs. We talked about it at lunch.

"I'm getting excused **early**," Becca said. "I work from 1 o'clock to 3 o'clock before the grade school kids go home."

"At the end of this week, I'll be an 𝔼𝕏ℙ𝔼ℝ𝕋 on saddles and bridles," Monica said. "I'm so excited!"

"Earth First took water samples all over the county," Peter said. "I have to test them for impurities." **He looked proud.**

"I'm going to watch the Hawks practice and write about it for the paper," Adam said. He made a "yes" gesture with his fist.

"A shipment of **new clothes** just arrived at Fiona's Fashions," Anna said, stopping at our table. "I get to dress the mannequins in new outfits."

"You're getting paid to **play with dolls**," Jenny said as she walked by.

"I'm designing a FABULOUS fashion display!" Anna said angrily. She turned on her heel and left.

I had no idea what Dad wanted me to do. I was nervous.

Monica knew a little about horse equipment, and Peter knew a lot about science. Adam knew as much as I did about baseball, and Anna was a fashion fanatic.

I didn't know much about computers. I could:

Send and read e-mails

Search for information

Play games

I wasn't a computer genius like my brother, but I wanted to learn. I was determined to become a valuable employee.

Luckily, I had a big advantage. **I already knew what drove my boss crazy.**

Only one thing annoyed Dad more than babbling: **Being late.**

When the last bell rang, I didn't dump my books in my locker. I dashed out the door with a full backpack.

It was 3 o'clock. I had to be at the store at 3:15. I jogged for a block, but then suddenly, I **had to slow down.**

I had to slow down because an elderly woman stood on the corner ahead of me. "Walter!" she called out. "Come here, right now."

A small dog bounded up to her. The woman bent over to grab his leash, but the dog was too quick. He barked and jumped back.

"**Walter!**" the woman shouted.

"Do you need help?" I asked.

"Yes, thank you," she said. "Walter is playing, and I'm too old to catch him."

I leaned over and held out my hand. "Hey, Walter. How are you doing, boy?" I asked the dog.

Walter jumped back and forth just out of my reach.

"Come on, boy," I said. "I'll scratch your ears. I bet you like having your ears scratched."

Walter bounced forward and jumped back several times. When he came close enough, I grabbed the leash.

"Gotcha!" I yelled. I handed Walter's leash to his owner. "I think he's **too tired** to play now," I told her.

The woman wanted to thank me, but I didn't have time to talk. I ran to Cortez Computers and pushed through the door at **3:20**. Dad was waiting.

"You're LATE, Claudia," he said. He frowned.

I didn't try to explain. I knew that Dad hated excuses almost as much as babbling and being late.

"I'm sorry. I'll stay ten minutes later to make up for it," I said.

"Okay," Dad agreed, "but I expect you to be on time tomorrow."

I had ruined my only chance to make **a great first impression**. I knew I couldn't make any more mistakes.

"Put your things in the storeroom," Dad said. "Then come to the front counter."

"Yes, sir," I said. I trudged to the storeroom and hurried back out.

Mr. Drake, one of my dad's employees, was showing laptops to a customer. They blocked the aisle.

Bad idea #1: I tried to squeeze past them.

There wasn't enough room. I bumped into a display of CD containers. Suddenly, the display started to topple.

Bad idea #2: I tried to stop it.

I opened my arms to hold the containers in place.

The display came tumbling down. CD containers hit the floor and rolled everywhere.

Mr. Drake and the customer jumped.

Dad came running right away. "What's going on?" he yelled.

Bad idea #3: I pretended the crash wasn't a problem.

"Don't worry, Dad," I said. I was on my knees to try to catch the runaway containers. "I've got it," I told him.

A container hit Dad's foot. He picked it up. The plastic was **broken**.

"Put the broken ones in the storeroom, Claudia," Dad said. "I'll fix the display."

I was so embarrassed. I didn't want to quit. I wanted a do-over. But since I couldn't go back in time, I had to settle for a do-better.

Soon, several people came in to buy computer parts and supplies.

Mr. Drake was still busy with the laptop customer, so I helped Dad at the checkout counter. He rang up sales on the cash register. I put the purchases in bags.

We were busy for an hour.

"You're very **polite** with the customers," Dad told me when things calmed down. "That's good."

I got a COMPLIMENT from my father! It was a jump-for-joy moment. But I kept my feet on the floor.

The fantastic feeling didn't last. Half an hour later, two customers came back in carrying Cortez Computers shopping bags.

"The printer ink I bought isn't in my bag," the first man said. "I have someone else's CD cases."

"The cases are mine," the second man said. "I have your ink cartridge. I drove all the way home before I found it."

"I'm so sorry," I said. **The mix-up was my fault.**

"That's all right," the first man said.

"Mistakes happen," the second man said. He took his cases and gave the first man his printer ink.

After they left, Dad looked at me. "I want to get new customers, Claudia," he said, **"not drive the old ones away."**

I felt terrible.

Good thing we didn't have a first-day employee evaluation. Mine would be a disaster.

1. Arrives late

2. Wrecks the merchandise

3. Annoys the customers

I had to become a better worker. **Otherwise, I might become the first Pine Tree Middle School seventh grader to flunk Work Week.**

REPORT CARD			
Claudia	7		
~~	-	-	
MATH	A		
ENGLISH	A		
SCIENCE	A		
WORKWEEK	F		

CHAPTER 6

FROM BAD TO WORSE

My bad day didn't end when I got home. First I had to walk a dog for one of my customers. Then I watched Nick while Mom made dinner. She did not pay me $2.00 an hour like she normally does.

"Keeping Nick busy helps you, Claudia," Mom said when I **complained**. "You eat dinner too. You shouldn't get paid to help me help you."

She had a point, but I had a point too.

"I have math homework," I said. "I can't watch Nick."

Mr. Chen was the **only teacher** who assigned homework. He said it was a life lesson. He told us, "Everyone works, and everyone has many other things to do. **You have algebra.**"

Mom agreed with **Mr. Chen**. I had algebra and Nick.

Nick followed me into the living room. "I'm **BORED**," he whined.

"Watch TV," I told him. I turned on cartoons and opened my math book.

Nick sat still for **one minute**. "I already saw this one," he complained.

I changed the channel.

"I hate this stupid **little kid stuff!**" Nick yelled. He jumped up and down on the sofa.

"Stop jumping!" I demanded.

"You can't make me!" Nick told me. He kept bouncing.

I stood up and put my hands on his shoulders. "Sit!" I said.

"Let go!" Nick screamed. "Let go!"

I let go.

"What do you want?" I asked.

"I want to play that blow-up ships game," Nick said.

"Battleship is a sink ships game," I said. "But I can't play. I have homework."

Nick folded his arms and glared at me.
"**I want to blow up ships!**" he yelled.

We played the game. I knew he wouldn't quiet down any other way.

Nick's mom picked him up at 6 o'clock. I took my homework upstairs. I sat at my desk and opened my algebra book.

Five minutes later, Mom called me for dinner. I hadn't finished **a single math problem**.

It was my turn to do the dishes. I didn't complain. I didn't want Dad to think I couldn't handle my job, my homework, and my chores, too.

At 8:30 p.m. I went back upstairs to do my homework. I didn't finish it until after 10.

The next morning, I woke up thirty minutes before my alarm went off. **I felt tired**, but I couldn't go back to sleep. I got ready for another long day.

Claudia's Weekday Morning Routine

1. Get dressed

2. Eat cereal, frozen waffles, or a cereal bar

3. Walk the dog who lives across the street

4. Walk to school

I dozed off during fourth period history class.

Monica poked me. "Wake up, Claudia," she  whispered.

"Huh?" I said. I sat up straight. For a second, I didn't know where I was. Anna reminded me.

"**Claudia fell asleep**, Ms. Stark," Anna announced. "Let her answer the question."

I didn't know the question!

"I have **a better idea**," Ms. Stark said. "Why don't you tell us how many amendments are in the Bill of Rights, Anna?"

Anna frowned.

I raised my hand. "Ten," I said.

"That's correct, Claudia," Ms. Stark said.

I stayed awake for the rest of the day, but **I was totally tired** when I got to the store.

When I walked in, Dad already had my  work day planned.

"The computer keeps track of everything we sell," Dad said. "But we take a weekly inventory to **double check** it."

"Okay," I said, nodding.

"Today I want you to count the items on the storeroom shelves," Dad said. "The inventory sheet is on the desk."

"Okay," I said. **I started to yawn.** I covered my mouth to hide it.

"I expect you to take this job seriously," Dad said.

"I do. HONEST," I said. I gave him my special I-really-mean-it look. Then I yawned.

Dad rolled his eyes. "I can't let you slide just because you're my daughter," he told me.

"I know," I said. Then I went to the storeroom before he started another lecture.

I began counting packs of copy paper. I was done with that, and counting packs of index cards when Dad came in.

"How are you doing?" Dad asked. He checked my inventory sheet and frowned. *"You're moving too slow,"* he told me.

"I'm being 𝔼𝕏𝕋ℝ𝔸 careful," I said.

That was only half true. I was **so tired** that I'd lost my place several times. So I had to start over.

"I have to leave on a service call," Dad said. He picked up his car keys. "Mr. Drake is here if you need him."

I was almost done counting when the phone rang. Mr. Drake was helping a customer, so I answered on the third ring. "Cortez Computers," I said. "This is Claudia."

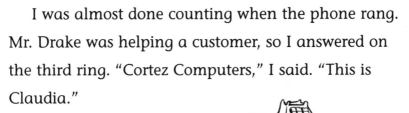

"Claudia, this is Jenny."

My stomach flip-flopped. Why was Jenny Pinski calling me? It couldn't be good. I must have made her mad, and **she was calling to threaten me!**

"We have a ℙℝ𝕆𝔹𝕃𝔼𝕄," Jenny said.

I had enough problems staying awake and keeping Dad happy. I couldn't deal with Jenny Pinski. I didn't even know what I had done to **make her mad!**

I didn't know what to do, so I hung up.

The phone rang again. I had to answer it. Otherwise, Mr. Drake would tell Dad I wasn't paying attention to business. I picked up the phone. "Cortez Computers, this is Claudia," I said nervously.

"You'd better **listen** to me, Claudia," Jenny said.

I hung up again. Jenny didn't call back. But my troubles weren't over.

Five minutes later, Nick's mom walked into the store. Nick was with her.

"Your mother said you'd watch him," Mrs. Wright said. "I have an appointment down the block. I'll be back in fifteen minutes."

"I don't like it here," Nick said.

"You have to stay anyway," I told him. I took a computer game down from the shelf.

Game makers always sent the store free demos of new games. They hoped Dad would order a hundred copies. He never did, though, not even when Jimmy loved a game.

"What's that?" Nick asked.

"A new game called **Planet Crusher**," I said.
"You'll love it." I loaded the game into the computer
on the storeroom desk. Nick sat down, and I went
back to counting.

It only took five minutes for Nick to
ruin my life.

"Uh-oh," Nick said nervously.

"What?" I asked. I jumped up. It was never good if
Nick was nervous.

"I was clicking e-mails and now they're gone,"
Nick said.

"Gone?" I repeated. I looked at the screen. Dad's
e-mail inbox was EMPTY. "Where are they?" I asked.

Nick shrugged. "I don't know," he said.

I didn't yell at him. Yelling wouldn't solve my
problem.

Instead, I picked up the phone. **I called my
brother in a panic.** He told me how to find my
father's missing e-mail.

Then I had to pay Nick a dollar to not tell my dad.

CHAPTER 7

F IS FOR FIRED

Everyone in the seventh grade had **jobs on the brain.** Some kids liked working and some didn't. At lunch, I figured out that there were three categories.

#1: It's So Cool I Can't Stand It!

"I wasn't sure I'd like being a reporter," Adam said.

My eyes POPPED with surprise. "But you knew you'd get to go to the Hawks' practice and meet the team!" I said. "How could you think you wouldn't like that?"

"I knew I'd love that," Adam said. "I didn't think I'd like writing about it."

"That's what reporters do," I said.

"Lucky for me!" Adam exclaimed. "I interviewed Mitch Watts, the **star pitcher.** He promised to autograph my newspaper article about him."

"I so wish I was you!" I said. I patted Adam on the back.

"My job at the movie theater is **tons better** than I thought, too," Carly said. "We can eat the old popcorn before we make a new batch."

"That's okay if you like popcorn," Anna grumbled.

"**I love popcorn.** Plus, I get to see a new movie for free every day," Carly said.

"I love being a **radio celebrity**," Tommy said proudly. "High school kids are calling my show. They like my jokes and the music I play."

"So do I," Becca said. She gazed at Tommy with **DREAMY** eyes. "Say your intro for me."

"Okay," Tommy said. He cleared his throat. "This is Tommy Talk on WHCR, the only place for CD chat, gossip gab, and every other teen topic that rocks your morning. You call. I'll answer. **Call now!**"

Becca giggled.

Anna rolled her eyes.

"I listen to you every day," Brad said.

That cinched it. Brad, Pine Tree Middle School's super popular sports star, liked the class clown's radio show. Tommy was a hit.

#2: Great Jobs With Little Glitches

"I love teaching second grade," Becca said. "The kids are making pictures to hang in the halls. We're having an art show, and I'm a judge."

"That sounds like FUN," Monica said.

"It is, mostly," Becca said. She sighed. "Nick Wright is in one of my classes."

"Did he kick you in the shins?" I asked.

Becca shook her head. "No," she told me. "He ate his crayons."

"He did that to gross you out," I told her.

"It worked," Becca said.

"I mostly like working at the Tack Shop," Monica said. "I love the smell of saddle leather and horse treats. And I'm learning a lot about grooming equipment and horse show gear."

"What don't you like?" Becca asked.

"Almost all our customers have a horse of their own," Monica said. "So do the other people who work at the store. I don't, and I wish I did. **I feel left out.** That makes my job hard."

"My job is hard too. Waitresses have to do a dozen things at once," Sylvia said. "I'm a good waitress, but only if I can **take my time.**"

"Is the Café owner mad at you?" Becca asked.

"No," Sylvia said. "But I only have two tables in my area, not four. So I only make half the tips."

"That's better than no tips," Monica said.

#3: Worse Than I Expected

"Testing water samples is boring," Peter  admitted. "I do the same thing over and over again. Put drops in a meter. Check the reading. Write the result by the sample number."

"But the lab uses the results to clean up unsafe water," I reminded him.

"True," Peter agreed, "but it's still 𝔹𝕆ℝ𝕀ℕ𝔾."

"**Boring** is better than hard," Brad said.

I usually stumble over my words when I talk to Brad. He looked so gloomy I decided to risk getting tongue-tied. "Working for the Hawks is FUN, isn't it?" I asked him.

"You get to hang out with the team every day," Adam said. "That must be fun!"

"I pour water and pick up equipment and hand out towels," Brad said. "I'm too busy and too tired to enjoy hanging out."

"That's not as bad as my stupid job," Anna said.

Everyone's heads snapped around.

A glob of macaroni and cheese fell off Tommy's fork. It went splat into his lap. He didn't notice. He just stared at Anna like the rest of us.

"You mean your job at Fiona's Fashions isn't AWESOME?" Carly asked. Nobody else dared ask Anna an embarrassing question.

"My job isn't glamorous or exciting," Anna complained. "I don't pick the outfits the mannequins wear. I just stuff them into the clothes. Their arms and legs are stiff, so it isn't easy."

"There must be **something good** about it," Carly said.

"There isn't," Anna snapped. "I have to put away the clothes customers try on and don't buy. And I got into trouble for being too 𝓗𝓞𝓝𝓔𝓢𝓣."

"How can you get into trouble for that?" I asked, raising an eyebrow.

"You can't tell a dumpy old lady she looks *fat and ridiculous*, even if she does," Anna said. "The customer went away mad, and Fiona was furious."

"I hate waiting on people too, but calling for repair service is worse," Jenny said. She glared at me. "When I called Cortez Computers for an appointment, **Claudia was rude.**"

#4: Joining The Ranks Of The Jobless

I was in category #4 by myself.

I was worse than rude when Jenny called the store yesterday. I had hung up on her. Twice!

Did my father know?

Yep.

Dad was waiting for me when I got to the store. He handed me an envelope. There was a pink piece of paper inside.

"What's this?" I asked.

"A pink slip," Dad said. "That's what a boss gives an employee that's being **fired**."

"I'm fired?" I whispered. **I was stunned.**

"You should be," Dad said. "You hung up on a customer yesterday. I almost lost the Million Movies account."

"I'm sorry," I said. "I didn't know —"

Dad cut me off. "I don't want to hear **explanations** or **excuses**," he said. "I'm giving the DVD store a big discount on a new monitor. They're giving me another chance."

I was glad to hear that, but I still felt awful. Dad shouldn't have to pay for something I did wrong. I had been *rude and irresponsible*, and he had every right to fire me.

If I Got Fired

1. My father would never trust or depend on me again.

2. Losing a job was an automatic F for the project.

3. I would be the only 7th grader ever to fail Work Week.

"I sent Jimmy to install the new monitor," Dad said. "Mr. Drake has the day off. I have computers to repair in back. So you have to watch the store. Call me when someone comes in."

I blinked. "I'm not fired?" I asked.

"Not this time," Dad said. "Everyone deserves a **second chance**, but you won't get a third."

I still had a job! I wanted to squeal and hug him, but that wasn't professional. After Dad closed the storeroom door, I jumped up and down happily.

Then I got to work. I dusted the computers. Then I straightened the shelves. When someone came in, I asked them to wait while I got Dad.

Dad ran credit cards, and I bagged the purchases. I made sure nothing got mixed up.

Jimmy called from Million Movies to report. The owner really liked the new flat-screen monitor. He ordered two more at full price for his other computers.

Dad was done being mad by the time I left the store. **That was good**, but it wasn't enough.

I only had three days left on the job. Then Dad would write my employee evaluation. He would be honest and fair.

He would write:

Claudia Cortez is late, clumsy, annoying, and rude.

I never give up, but I had made so many awful mistakes. **Was it too late to make my dad proud?**

CHAPTER 8

BRAINSTORM

Dad didn't say another word about my monitor mistake. Not at dinner or breakfast or when I got to work Thursday afternoon.

Sometimes silence is worse than a lecture. I didn't know what Dad was thinking. I had to guess.

The Mysterious Mind of Eduardo Cortez

Was he:

A. So disappointed he wanted to forget anything had happened?

B. Wishing Work Week was over so he'd never see me in the store again?

C. Hoping there were no more major mess-ups?

D. All of the above.

The answer was probably D. I knew I couldn't mess up again.

* * *

"I have a meeting with a **new client**," Dad said when I arrived at the store after school. "Mr. Drake will take care of the customers. I want you to unpack some boxes."

"Okay," I said.

"Check EVERYTHING against the packing list," Dad said.

"What's the packing list?" I asked.

"A list of everything that's in the box," Dad explained. "Or **should be** in the box."

I counted and matched computer parts for half an hour. I put a check mark by every item on the packing list. I looked up when **Mr. Drake** walked into the storeroom.

"Watch the front door for a few minutes, Claudia," Mr. Drake said. "I have *a big sale customer*. He wants a complete computer package."

"Okay," I said. I got up and headed into the front of the store.

I wasn't finished unpacking, but customers come first. I sat behind the front counter and watched the door.

My first customer was **trying not to cry.**

"I'm so upset," the woman said. "I borrowed this laptop from my son. It was working fine last night, but now it won't turn on. Did I 𝐵𝑅𝐸𝐴𝐾 it?"

I didn't know. Mr. Drake was busy, and Dad was at a meeting. The woman looked so frantic **I had to do something.**

I called Jimmy. "I have a question," I said.

"I don't have an answer," Jimmy said. **"I'm busy."** My brother only talked to me when it's absolutely necessary. But I was a little sister. I knew how to get to him.

#1: Just keep talking

"My customer's laptop won't turn on," I said.

"Make sure the battery is snapped in right," Jimmy said. "Sometimes you have to **snap it in.**"

"Okay," I said.

I removed the battery and snapped it back into place. I pushed the power button. The laptop powered up right away.

"Thank you so much!" the woman said. She grinned. "How much do I owe you?"

I couldn't charge for a two-second phone call. "It's free," I said. "We just want to **keep our customers happy**."

"*I'm thrilled,*" the woman said. She bought printer paper, a crossword puzzle computer game, and headphones.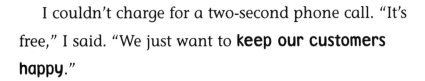

Mr. Drake left his customer for a few minutes. He needed to run the cash register. When the woman was gone, he showed me how to do it. "You can handle cash and checks, Claudia," he told me. "**Call me** if someone wants to use a credit card."

The next customer asked for my dad.

"He's not here," I said. "Can I help?"

"I don't think so," the man said. "My computer is running slow, and **it's driving me crazy**."

"We might be able to fix that," I said. "I'll ask our on-call **expert**."

I quickly called Jimmy.

"I have another customer," I said when my brother answered the phone. "His computer is running slow. I told him you could fix it."

I gave the phone to the customer. Jimmy asked questions, and the man took notes.

"*That's all*? Download a clean-up program?" the customer asked. Then he thanked Jimmy and gave the phone back to me. "Is there a charge?" he asked.

"No charge," I told him. "Jimmy's advice is 𝔽ℝ𝔼𝔼 for our customers."

"That's great!" the man said. He bought batteries and a portable DVD player for his daughter's birthday. He wanted to pay with a credit card. I called Mr. Drake over.

I stayed late to finish unpacking. I put everything on the storeroom shelves and flattened the boxes. Then I put the packing lists on Dad's desk.

Mr. Drake stopped me on my way out.

"You had **good sales** today, Claudia!" Mr. Drake exclaimed. **"What's your secret?"**

Mr. Drake was joking, but it gave me a brilliant idea.

I smiled and told him, **"Ask Jimmy."**

CHAPTER 9

ASK JIMMY

Friday morning smelled like Saturday. Mom was cooking bacon, scrambled eggs, and toast.

I was STARVING when I ran downstairs. But Mrs. Wright had an early charity event that morning. And Mom was watching Nick.

NICK NOTE: Never eat breakfast with Nick. Nick gulps his milk and chews with his mouth open.

Then Mom said I had to walk him to school.

Nick didn't care if he was late for school. He **walked slow** and kept stopping to look at things.

I couldn't be late. Nothing had gone wrong at school or work the day before. Nothing could go wrong today. Dad had given me a second chance. But he had made it clear that **I wouldn't get a third**.

"Have you seen the new **Viper Man** movie yet?" I asked Nick.

"No," Nick said. "I have to go like this every time someone talks about it." He closed his eyes and covered his ears. Then he sang loudly, **"La–la–la!"**

"I'll take you to see it," I said. "But only if you get to school before the bell rings."

Nick 𝓑𝓞𝓛𝓣𝓔𝓓 down the sidewalk.

I made it to Homeroom with forty-one seconds to spare. The rest of the day dragged. For the first time, I couldn't wait to get to the store.

I hoped my idea would keep old customers and help get new ones. That's what my father/boss wanted. It was the only way I could earn **a good employee evaluation.**

I didn't see my father when I walked in. "Where's Dad?" I asked Mr. Drake.

"He's getting the new client's order together," Mr. Drake explained.

"What should I do?" I asked.

"Let's finish your **on-the-job training,**" Mr. Drake told me.

He taught me how to use the credit card machine. When we were done, **I sprang into action.**

I took two signs out of my backpack. I put one in the window and one on the counter. They said:

Got a computer problem?

Ask Jimmy!

A free service for all our customers.

The night before, I had convinced Jimmy to work with me. He was home playing a computer game anyway. If my plan was a bust, he wouldn't lose anything. If it worked, **everyone would win.**

Our first two customers bought supplies. Then a high school kid came in. He had a computer game and a complaint.

"This game won't run," he said.

"That's a problem for Jimmy. He knows all about games," I said. I dialed the phone and handed it to the boy.

"It's *Auto Maverick 2.0*," the kid told Jimmy. "I bought it on sale last week."

He and Jimmy talked for a while. Then the boy handed the phone back to me.

"Did Jimmy help?" I asked.

"**I hope so**," the boy said. "He told me to update the video card drivers. I can download them **online for free**."

He didn't buy anything. But he promised to come back for the next end-of-the-month sale.

Jimmy couldn't solve the next person's problem **over the phone**. The man needed a repair appointment. Mr. Drake set it up.

"**Ask Jimmy** is a fantastic idea, Claudia," Mr. Drake told me. He was impressed. "You've earned your pay this week."

I hoped Dad thought so too. He was still busy with the new account. I left before he finished.

SUPER SELLER

Dad left for work before I came downstairs Saturday morning.

"He's setting up computers for **a new customer**," Mom explained.

Jimmy dropped me off at the store later that day.

"Will you be home if a customer needs help?" I asked.

"Not today, Claudia," Jimmy said. **"Sorry."**

I took my signs down and put them behind the counter.

"Jimmy's earned *a day off*," Mr. Drake said. "And it's okay. **Simon** is here."

The Good Thing: Simon Fitch goes to college. He works on Saturdays, and he knows a lot about computers. He could handle customers with problems.

The Bad Thing: I couldn't show Dad how well Ask Jimmy worked. Mr. Drake would tell him about it on Monday, but then I wouldn't be there and **Work Week** would be over.

Cortez Computers was very busy on Saturdays. Mr. Drake and Simon helped people on the floor. I ran the cash register and answered the phone. We were **swamped** when Dad finally came back. I had three customers lined up.

"Need some help?" Dad asked. He didn't look **SURPRISED** to see me behind the counter by myself.

"Yes, please!" I said. I started to move over so that Dad could work the register and I could bag the purchases.

"Stay there," Dad said. "I'll bag."

I was shocked. Dad trusted me to make change and run credit cards! I paid extra close attention. I didn't want to make a mistake.

The phone rang. Dad smiled when he hung up. "That was a customer. He called to **thank us** for helping him get a game to run," he said.

"Jimmy did it," I said.

"Yes," Dad agreed, "but only because you started the store's **Ask Jimmy** problem-solving service."

I gasped. "You know about it?" I asked.

"Mr. Drake told me," Dad said. "It's a BRILLIANT idea, Claudia. And you're a **terrific** salesperson."

"I am?" I asked. I was shocked again.

"You sold a portable DVD player and several other things yesterday," Dad said. "That's great. **You're doing a wonderful job, Claudia.**"

I couldn't believe it. My father was so proud he was gushing with praise!

The door opened. An elderly woman walked in carrying a small dog. "**There you are!**" she said. "Walter and I have been looking for you."

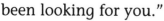

Dad raised an eyebrow. "Is Walter the dog?" he asked.

"My NAUGHTY dog," the woman said. She smiled at me. "You were so nice to help me catch him on Monday. I want to give you a reward."

"I don't need a reward," I said. **"I was glad to help."**

"Is that why you were late?" Dad asked.

"Yes," I admitted. "I didn't tell you because I didn't want to **make excuses** on my first day."

"That's my girl," Dad said. He smiled proudly.

"Well, I want to return the favor," the old woman said. "I need a new computer, so **I'll buy it here.**"

Dad and I both stared at her, shocked.

"My family wants me to get e-mail," the woman explained. "I'm not quite sure what e-mail is."

"Don't worry," Dad said. "You can **Ask Jimmy**. He'll teach you everything you need to know. There's no charge."

Dad left to help her pick out a computer. He looked back, gave me a thumbs-up, and winked.

I almost fell over. My dad never winked unless he was really, really happy! **It was the best employee evaluation ever.**

CHAPTER 11

P.S.

I didn't get a PERFECT employee evaluation. I was late the first day, and I had made a couple of serious mistakes. But I had also improved a lot. Dad wrote in his report that he wanted to *hire me* when I turned sixteen, just like Jimmy.

Ms. Stark gave me an **A-** for the project. Dad gave me the commission for the computer sale to Walter's owner. That was almost a hundred dollars! He also gave me a bonus for my **Ask Jimmy** idea. The extra money was way more than I needed to take Nick to the movies.

Dad is paying Jimmy $5.00 for every problem he solves on the phone. He's also paying for a cell phone. That way Jimmy can be reached **anywhere,** anytime. My brother is thrilled.

My friends enjoyed **Work Week**, but they don't want the same jobs when they grow up. Except Tommy. He wants to be a stand-up comedian, a sitcom actor, and a radio host.

Anna **never** wants to work for someone else. She wants to be her own boss, just like I do. So she'll have to start her own company just like me. Can you believe it? **Anna Dunlap and I finally agree on something!**

Diana G. Gallagher lives in Florida with her husband and five dogs, four cats, and a cranky parrot. Her hobbies are gardening, garage sales, and grandchildren. She has been an English equitation instructor, a professional folk musician, and an artist. However, she had aspirations to be a professional writer at the age of twelve. She has written dozens of books for kids and young adults.

About the Illustrator

Brann Garvey lives in Minneapolis, Minnesota with his wife, Keegan, their dog, Lola, and their very fat cat, Iggy. Brann graduated from Iowa State University with a bachelor of fine arts degree. He later attended the Minneapolis College of Art and Design, where he studied illustration. In his free time, Brann enjoys being with his family and friends. He brings his sketchbook everywhere he goes.

Glossary

announcements (uh-NOUNSS-muhnts)—messages spoken publicly

applied (uh-PLYED)—asked for a job

auditioned (aw-DISH-uhnd)—tried out for a part

employed (em-PLOID)—having a job

employee (em-PLOI-ee)—a person who works for someone else

employer (em-PLOI-ur)—someone who is the boss of other people

evaluation (i-val-yoo-AY-shuhn)—a description of how well someone did

experience (ek-SPEER-ee-uhnss)—knowledge and skill that you gain by doing something

hire (HIRE)—to give someone a job

interview (IN-tur-vyoo)—a meeting at which someone is asked questions

inventory (IN-vuhn-tor-ee)—a list of items

professional (pruh-FESH-uh-nuhl)—behaving appropriately and politely

references (REF-uh-renss-iz)—people who can be asked about a person's skills and qualifications for a job

résumé (RE-zuh-may)—a list of the jobs and education a person has

Discussion Questions

1. Talk about the jobs that different students have in this book. What other jobs are available in your community? What job would you choose?

2. Why is Anna mean to the other students? What are some good ways to handle a bully?

3. Claudia comes up with a service, Ask Jimmy, that helps her father's store. What else could she have done to make a good impression to her boss?

Writing Prompts

1. What job do you want to have when you're an adult? Write about it.

2. Claudia is jealous that her father is proud of Jimmy's work at Cortez Computers. Write about a time you were jealous of someone. What were you jealous about? How did you stop feeling jealous?

3. Design a poster advertising Cortez Computers and the Ask Jimmy service. Then write a newspaper article that describes Ask Jimmy.

MORE FUN with Claudia!

POOL PROBLEM

THE COMPLICATED LIFE OF

Claudia
Cristina
Cortez

BY DIANA G. GALLAGHER

Claudia Cristina Cortez

Just like every other thirteen-year-old girl, Claudia Cristina Cortez has a complicated life. Whether she's studying for the big Quiz Show, babysitting her neighbor, Nick, avoiding mean Jenny Pinski, planning the seventh-grade dance, or trying desperately to pass the swimming test at camp, Claudia goes through her complicated life with confidence, cleverness, and a serious dash of cool.

David Mortimore Baxter

David is a great kid, but he has one big problem — he can't stop talking. These wildly humorous stories, told by David himself, will show readers just how much trouble a boy and his mouth can get into, whether he's going on a class trip, trying to find a missing neighbor, running a detective agency, or getting lost in the wild. David is amiable, engaging, cool, and smart enough to realize that growing up is the biggest adventure of all.